Resistance

by

Ann Jungman

Illustrated by Alan Marks

To Kathryn
with love

First published in 2002 in Great Britain by
Barrington Stoke Ltd, Sandeman House, Trunk's Close,
55 High Street, Edinburgh EH1 1SR

Reprinted 2003, 2004

ISBN 1-84299-047-0

Printed by Polestar Wheatons Ltd

MEET THE AUTHOR - ANN JUNGMAN

What is your favourite animal?
Wolf
What is your favourite boy's name?
Guy
What is your favourite girl's name?
Abigail
What is your favourite food?
Beef stroganoff
What is your favourite music?
Bob Dylan and Mozart
What is your favourite hobby?
Cinema and cooking

MEET THE ILLUSTRATOR - ALAN MARKS

What is your favourite animal?
A snow leopard
What is your favourite boy's name?
Thomas
What is your favourite girl's name?
Kate
What is your favourite food?
Oysters
What is your favourite music?
Mozart
What is your favourite hobby?
Cooking

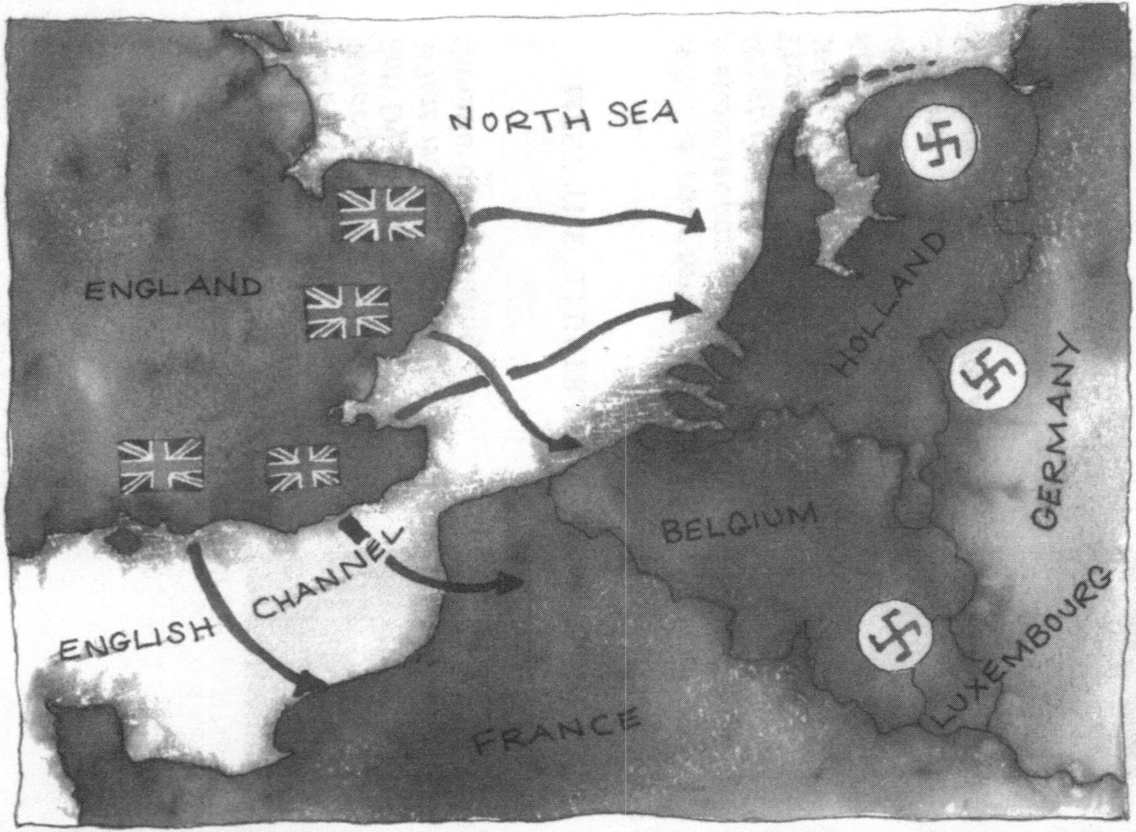
NORTH SEA
ENGLAND
HOLLAND
GERMANY
BELGIUM
ENGLISH CHANNEL
LUXEMBOURG
FRANCE

Contents

Chapter 1
Major Konrad

"Check mate," cried Major Konrad triumphantly. "I've beaten you at chess yet again, Bakker. You need to practise, my friend. And to think what you are doing."

"With all the practice in the world, Major, I could never beat you at chess. You are out of my class. If there wasn't a war on, you would be a world grandmaster."

Jan clenched his fists. He had been watching his father and the Major finish their game. He knew that his father could beat the German officer any time. But he just let him win.

Jan knew why his father did this. It was because they were Dutch and the country had been occupied by the Germans. Jan's father worked for the Germans and the Major could help him. It was worth making a friend of him.

Out of the corner of his eye, Jan saw his mother slam the kettle down on the stove.

"Are you making coffee, Mrs Bakker?" asked Major Konrad.

"Yes," she replied. "Not real coffee, of course. This is the rubbish we Dutch have to make do with. It's made from acorns and goodness knows what. Would you like a cup?"

"Ah, but I have a little present for you," he said with a smile and pulled a small package out of his pocket. "Some real coffee with the compliments of the German government." The Major clicked his heels and smiled.

Jan watched his mother take the package. She said nothing. Soon the room was filled with the rich smell of real coffee. His mouth watered as his mother took the boiling kettle off the stove and went to get cups from the shelf. To his amazement, she only got out two cups.

"You are not having any then, Mrs Bakker?" asked Major Konrad.

"No, Major, it will only keep me awake and Jan too. The young need their sleep. Now off to bed, Jan, school tomorrow."

"But mother," protested Jan as she pushed him out of the kitchen, "I love coffee, you know I do. And so do you."

"No-one else in this town or indeed in Holland is drinking real coffee just now. So we can do without it too," she replied. There was anger in her voice. "Now don't argue, just go to bed." She gave him a kiss.

Jan lay in his bed and shivered. It was cold outside and there was very little coal to heat the houses. *I wish all this was over,* he thought, *I wish the Germans would get out of Holland so that things could get back to normal.* He smiled as he remembered what fun life had been before the war.

Outside he could hear Major Konrad leaving. Jan pulled back his curtain and looked out.

"Heil Hitler," cried Major Konrad, raising his arm in the Nazi salute.

"Heil Hitler," replied his father, clicking his heels together and raising his arm.

Jan looked across the street and saw other people glowering from their windows. Jan climbed back into his bed and thought to himself, *Even when this awful war is over, it won't be over for us. Everyone hates us.*

It was like this all the time. Jan just wished his father hadn't decided to help the Germans and join the Nazi police.

Chapter 2
School

"Jan!" shouted his mother. "Hurry up. You know how angry Miss Hals gets if you're late for school."

Jan picked up his schoolbag but he did not hurry. His heart sank as he set off down the road, walking very slowly. School was hell these days. He wondered how long it would be before trouble started.

It didn't take long. A boy in his class, Pieter, stepped out from a side-lane and walked along beside him.

"And how did you enjoy your *real* coffee last night?" he asked.

"I didn't drink any coffee," mumbled Jan.

Another boy, Willem, had come up on the other side of Jan. "Oh, so it was just Mummy and Daddy drinking coffee with the nice German officer, was it?" he sneered.

Then Willem grabbed Jan's bag and flung it as far as he could over a fence. The three boys stood and watched as the bag flew through the air and landed just short of the canal.

"I can't believe you're doing this. You used to be my friends," said Jan.

"That was before your dad decided to work for the Germans and my dad was carted off to the work camps in Germany," said Willem.

"It's a pity the bag didn't fall in the canal," said Pieter. "Oh, well, better luck next time, Willem. Then our Nazi-loving friend would be in real trouble with Miss Hals."

Jan sighed, climbed over the fence and picked up his bag. *I'll be late for school again,* he thought.

But he didn't really mind. He hated school these days. No-one would speak to him. It had got much worse now that the children's fathers had vanished. No-one knew if they were alive or dead. No wonder the other children hated Jan. There was no way *his* father was going to be sent to Germany.

Just as he came near the school, the town clock struck eight.

"Late again, Jan Bakker," said Miss Hals looking down her nose at him. "Third time in a week. As a punishment, you can stay behind after school and clean up. You won't mind as there will be a nice hot cup of *real* coffee waiting for you when you get home."

"Mother and I didn't drink any of that coffee," Jan told her angrily. "Mother says if no-one else in Holland can have coffee, then we shouldn't either."

"I see," said Miss Hals. "Well, well. But you will have to stay in after school, Jan, anyway. You've been late just too many times."

As always, Jan sat at the back of the room. No-one spoke to him. No-one looked at him. It was as if he wasn't there at all.

Then the door opened and Elli Wessel was firmly pushed into the room by her mother. Elli's eyes were red. Jan was surprised to see her at all.

Elli hardly ever came to school any more. She was always off sick. Jan wondered if it was because her father, like his father, was in the Nazi Police. She, too, was teased and bullied by the others.

As Elli walked through the class to the back of the room, all the others looked down at their desks, as if she didn't exist.

Elli sat down next to Jan. He reached out and touched her arm.

Elli smiled at him, dried her eyes and wrote him a note:

I can't stand the silence any more. No-one will talk to me

Jan wrote underneath:

> I know. I feel the same, but be brave.
> We haven't done anything wrong and the war
> will be over soon

Elli wrote back:

> It will never be over for
> us. People will never forgive
> anyone who was on the side of
> the Nazis

Suddenly their teacher was standing over them. "So what have we here? Our two outcasts writing notes to each other." Then she grabbed the paper and read it quickly.

Her face softened. "Oh," she said sadly, "your fathers do deals with the Nazis and you pay the price. The rest of us don't understand how hard it must be for you, Jan and Elli. We just don't want to know."

Chapter 3
Strike

After school, Jan followed Elli out of the building. "Shall I walk you home?" he asked.

"Why?" she asked.

"Well, to make sure you get home safely and so you'll have someone to talk to."

"It's awful, isn't it," said Elli, "this wall of silence that tells us how much we are hated."

Jan nodded and at that moment a storm of snowballs began to fall on them. This was not a snowball fight between friends. It was hard and hurtful.

There were shouts of: "Traitors!" and "Nazi lovers!"

Jan stood in front of Elli and tried to protect her. When the storm of snowballs stopped, they both brushed the snow off their coats and faces.

"Thank you, Jan, thank you for trying to protect me," said Elli, trying not to cry.

"It's nothing, Elli, the least I could do."

"I'm glad you're still my friend. And I'm yours," she told him with a brave smile.

"That'll keep us going," he replied.

When Jan got home, he could hear his father banging his fist on the table and

shouting at his mother. "They're crazy,
I tell you, they're crazy. Nothing good will
come of this."

Jan wondered what this was all about.

"Calm down, Willem," said Jan's mother,
"there are more important things to think
about. The war is nearly over and you know
it. Then we will all have to pay the price for
your being on the wrong side. All those who
have been too friendly with the Germans will
go to prison and what will happen to Jan
and me?"

"Don't say such things. The Germans
haven't lost the war yet. People get shot for
saying that," shouted his father.

"What's happened?" asked Jan, taking off
his wet coat.

"All the railwaymen are going on strike.
Our Queen has broadcast on the radio from

London, telling them to cripple the railway system. There'll be no trains going anywhere in Holland."

"Why?" demanded Jan.

"So the Germans can't move men and weapons around."

"What will happen to the railwaymen?" demanded Jan.

"They'll be sent to prison," his father told him. "And the leaders may be shot."

"I've been told that they've all gone into hiding," said his mother, "they've found shelter in farms all over Holland."

"So what will the Germans do?" asked Jan.

"They are going to cut off our supplies of coal and food," said his mother. "It looks like being a long, hard winter. We shall have no heating or electricity and very little food."

"How will we manage?" asked Jan.

"We'll have to get wood from the forests and food wherever we can," his mother told him. "The farmers won't give *us* any food. Everyone knows that your father is on the side of the Germans. It's going to be a hard winter for everyone but even worse for us. Unless the Major brings us more of his little presents."

Chapter 4
In the Woods

As the strike bit, it got harder and harder to get food to eat or wood for the fire. Everyone was hungry and cold and at school, the children wore all the clothes they had. The older boys had vanished. Some had been sent to Germany to work in the factories and mines. Others had gone into hiding.

Every day and night, British and American planes flew over the town on their way to bomb Germany. Their droning noise kept the children awake.

"The war has to be nearly over," Jan said to Elli one day when they were deep in the forest searching for wood.

"My mother listens to the London radio. The BBC is saying that the Americans and the British have landed in France and that they'll soon be here," she told him.

"It's a crime to listen to the BBC," Jan said. "You must be careful."

"The Germans don't worry about us children or our mums," replied Elli. "They think the whole family must be on their side. After all, our fathers have joined the Nazi police."

"So, we're Nazi lovers too, are we?" asked Jan.

"Well, are we?" said Elli and she turned and looked at him hard in the eye. "Do you really want the Germans to win this war? They bomb our towns, they take our men away, they starve us, they put anyone who speaks up against them in prison or they shoot them. How do you feel Jan, how do you *really* feel?"

Jan tramped along next to her thinking hard. "You're right, Elli. I hate the Germans. Our fathers made a wrong choice, a stupid and wicked choice. They joined the Nazis. But this doesn't mean that we have to go along with them, does it?"

"No, Jan, but what can we do about it?"

"Nothing," agreed Jan sadly. "The Resistance Movement wouldn't have anything to do with us. They'd think we might betray them."

"That's right," agreed Elli, "but that doesn't mean we can't fight the Nazis in our own way."

"What do you mean?" asked Jan. "I don't understand."

"Just think a moment," said Elli. "Which children in our class can get hold of information that would be useful to the Resistance?"

"Us, I suppose," said Jan in surprise.

"Exactly. When Major Konrad and the other Nazis come to our house, they tell my father all sorts of things."

"Yes!" cried Jan catching on to Elli's idea. "My father often tells my mother what's been happening up at the Nazi Headquarters and what the German plans are. Mostly I don't bother to listen, but I could. But Elli, if we can't give the information to the Resistance because no-one would believe us or trust us, who *can* we tell?"

"We'll have to work that one out," said Elli.

Just then, they saw through the trees an old, deserted hut. The door was hanging open and the roof was falling in. They stopped and stared.

"Did you know there was a deserted hut here in the woods?" whispered Jan.

Elli shook her head. "Hush, it's not deserted at all. Look – someone is coming out."

Chapter 5
In Hiding

The two of them crouched behind a tree and watched. A man and a girl came out, very thin, their clothes torn and shabby. They were picking things up off the ground.

"They're looking for mushrooms," whispered Jan.

As the pair got nearer, Jan drew his breath in sharply. Elli looked at him but said nothing.

As soon as the pair were out of sight, Elli asked, "Who are they? Do you know them?"

"Of course I do. It's Dr Stein, our dentist, and his daughter Ruth who used to be in our class."

"I didn't live here then," Elli reminded him. "Are they Jews?"

Jan nodded, "Yes, they vanished. People said they had gone to England or America."

"There will be a reward for anyone who tells the Germans where they are. The Nazi Police offer good money to people who betray Jews and who give them the names of people who help them."

"Elli, you wouldn't ..."

"No, of course not, but more and more people are coming here to look for food and wood. The Steins will be found out."

Just then, they heard the sound of voices and crouched behind some bushes.

"Dr Stein, you must not wander into the woods, it's not safe," said a familiar voice. "I've got you some milk and a bit of fish and bread. It's not much, but it's the best I can do. We're all hungry and you don't have ration books."

Jan began to shake. It was Pieter – the boy from his class who tormented him daily. Pieter, whose father had been shot for being in the Resistance, and who was now risking his own life hiding and feeding Jews.

"You're right, Pieter," said Dr Stein. He sounded very tired. "But we need some fresh air and to stretch our legs, as well as some mushrooms and roots to eat."

"But you can't risk your life and Ruth's too. The war must be ending soon. The British and Americans are in France, they've reached southern Holland. Be patient just a bit longer."

"Pieter, it's not that we aren't grateful. There are no words to say how grateful we are. But we can't stand living in this hide-out much longer," Ruth sighed.

"Look – I've brought you some books," Pieter told her. "I know how you love to read. And here's a pack of cards. It's the best I can do. Stay here till it gets dark. The Germans are searching the farms today for food and for men to work in their camps. After dark, go to the Groots' farm, there you can get warm and get some sleep and eat something hot."

"And have a bath?" asked Ruth with a smile.

"Not much chance," replied Pieter, "it's hard to get hot water these days. There is no power any more because the electricity stations have run out of coal."

"Just when you think it can't get any worse, it does," groaned Ruth.

"I know," grinned Pieter. "But it's nearly over, I promise."

"People have been saying that for months," sighed Ruth.

"Yes, but this time it's true," said her father. "Look at the planes overhead. They're all British or American and they're bombing Germany. Soon the Nazis will have to give in, just you see."

Chapter 6
Resistance

Jan sat in the kitchen and sipped his carrot and potato soup and stared into space.

"It's the best I can do," snapped his mother. "You can't get meat or bread anywhere. Just be grateful it's hot. When our coal runs out you'll be eating cold food."

Just then, Jan heard the sound of an axe chopping wood. He ran to the window and there was his father, in the garden, cutting down their only apple tree.

"Dad, no!" he shouted. "I love that tree! I used to climb that tree when I was little and swing on it. And we can eat the apples."

"Too bad," his father shouted back. "We need to keep warm. You can't get upset about a tree these days. You'd better come and help me, I'm expecting Major Konrad any minute."

"I'll just finish my soup first," called Jan. He sipped away as slowly as he could. Soon there was the sound of a motorbike and Major Konrad strode in.

Jan's father came in from the garden, mopping his forehead.

"Well, Bakker, get into your uniform quickly. We have been given information that there are young men hiding in the woods near the old, deserted hut. Who knows, maybe they're Resistance fighters or Jews? So be at Police Headquarters at midday. We're going to search those woods like they've never been searched before and we'll need all the men we can get."

Jan lowered his head and began to hum. He pretended he wasn't listening.

"Mid-day it is, Major. Heil Hitler!" cried Jan's father.

"Heil Hitler!" replied the Major.

Jan thought quickly. "Mum, I feel sick. I can't work on that tree right now."

"All right, Jan," said his mother, feeling his head. "You do feel hot. You'd better lie down for a bit."

Jan stumbled upstairs, got undressed and let his mother tuck him up in bed.

As soon as she was gone, he grabbed a piece of paper and wrote on it:

> They are going to search the woods near you today. Go and hide on the other side of the river.
> A friend

Then he got dressed again, climbed out of his window and ran towards the woods. When he got near to the deserted hut, he stopped and picked up a stone.

He wrapped the note round the stone and from behind a tree threw it at the window.

The glass smashed. *They must have heard it*, Jan thought, and he turned round and raced home before anyone saw him.

Jan climbed back through the window of the room, his heart thumping. Will they take any notice? Or will they think it's a prank? Did I get there in time?

When his mother brought him more soup on a tray for lunch, he decided he would rather be downstairs where he would hear any news. "I'm feeling better, Mum. I'd rather eat at the table."

"Just as you like," replied his mother.

So Jan sat in the kitchen all day wrapped in three coats and some blankets, shaking with fear, as he waited for news.

At last his father came in and slammed the door. *They didn't find them,* thought Jan, *or he'd be in a better mood.*

Jan's father threw his gloves down on the table and began to undo his snow-covered boots. "We searched all afternoon in that freezing wood for nothing," he growled.

"It serves you right, if you're frozen. Hunting people like animals. You should be ashamed," commented his wife.

"But they're not people – Jews and Resistance workers are rats," he replied. "Anyway, someone has been living in the hut not so long ago. There are still the remains of a fire and food in there."

"Maybe someone warned them," suggested Jan's mother.

"No way," sneered his father. "No-one but the Police and the Germans knew we were going to search the wood."

Jan sank deeper into the mountain of clothes he was wearing and pretended to be asleep.

"Anyway, whoever it was in that deserted hut has got away," said his father. "For the moment, that is."

Chapter 7
Elli

On the way to school the next day, Jan saw Elli up ahead. He ran to catch up with her. "Hey, Elli, I did it, I did what you suggested," he told her smiling.

"Whatever are you talking about?" Elli asked.

"I was in the kitchen yesterday when Major Konrad came to tell my dad that they

43

were going to search the woods. I went and warned the Steins."

Elli stopped and looked at him with huge eyes. "You warned them?"

Jan nodded.

"And the Steins listened to you?"

"Well, no, not exactly. I wrote a note, I didn't sign it of course, wrapped it round a stone and chucked it through the window."

"Jan, that was brilliant, brilliant. I'm so proud of you."

"Look at the lovebirds," came Pieter's voice.

"Jan loves Elli, Jan loves Elli," chanted the others.

"Take no notice," Elli told Jan, though she blushed a deep red. Then she took his arm. Jan noticed that she was standing up tall and that she held her head high for the first time that he could remember.

"We need to plan. Let's meet after school."

So after school, he went over to Elli's house.

"Be back before the curfew," said his mother. "We don't want you to be arrested for being out after dark."

"You're a bit young to be going with girls, aren't you?" commented his father.

"Leave the boy alone. He needs friends," said Mrs Bakker. "It's hard on Jan and me to be hated by everyone because of your crazy views. No-one will talk to us. Elli is the only friend Jan has at the moment, so let him be."

Jan smiled at his mother and ran out of the door.

As he ran, he didn't notice a gang of boys coming towards him. One of them put out his foot and tripped Jan up. He fell flat on his face in the hard snow.

The other boys laughed as Jan got to his feet and limped on to Elli's house.

When he got there, Elli dragged him up to the bathroom and washed the scratches on his hands and elbows.

"I wish it was all over, Elli," sighed Jan. "It just goes on and on."

"But Jan, don't you see? It's good. If the others bully us like this, no-one else is going to suspect what we're doing. Now that you've found a way of using the information you get at home, we might become suspects. The worse the others treat us, the less likely anyone is to find out that we've changed sides."

"You're so clever, Elli," said Jan nodding.

"Have you heard anything new today?"

Elli shook her head, "No, nothing. They're very angry at being made to look silly searching the woods with so many people and finding no-one. They have no new plans at the moment."

"I think the Germans know that things are going badly for them. It's only a matter of months, maybe weeks, before the British or American soldiers get here."

"I know," agreed Elli. "But we must try and see that no-one else gets killed before they get here."

"We're part of the Resistance, aren't we, Elli?" smiled Jan. "In our own way."

"We are," she smiled back. "We are. We're our very own Resistance Movement. There's only two of us, but we're playing a very important part."

Chapter 8
Hunger

Jan looked at his family sitting huddled round the tiny log fire. The cooking pot hung over it. They were all wrapped in blankets and shivering as his mother stirred the soup.

Jan couldn't remember such a hard winter. They had no gas, no electricity, very little fuel and almost no food.

"Your friends the Germans," said Jan's mother bitterly, "keep punishing us all the time. We have so little food that some people are slowly starving to death."

"Don't start that again," replied her husband.

"At least we still have something to eat," Jan's mother said, as she handed him a plate with a few potatoes and something Jan hadn't seen before floating in water.

"What's this, Mum?" he asked.

"Better not know," she replied. "Just be glad we've got something we can eat."

"They look like onions but they're not," went on Jan.

"Your mother is giving us tulip bulbs to eat," said his father. "That's all we can get."

Jan forced himself to eat this soup. It was revolting. "It tastes good," he lied.

Just then Private Stern came in with another soldier. "Sorry to bother you, Bakker, but the Major wants you at Headquarters."

Jan listened hard. Maybe he could find out what was going on.

"Is it something important?" he asked Private Stern.

Private Stern sighed, "No, Jan, nothing exciting, just some more arrests."

This man must be nearly sixty, Jan thought. *The new troops coming from Germany are either old like him or very young like the soldier who's come with him.* Jan decided that this one was probably only a year or so older than him. *Things must be bad in Germany if they're sending grandfathers and schoolboys to war*, thought Jan.

"Mrs Bakker, I regret to tell you that we have orders to search every house. We need to make sure that there are no Resistance fighters hiding in your home. We are also looking for fit young men who might be avoiding service in German work camps," said Private Stern.

"But my husband is in the Nazi Police. You can't suspect us of hiding anyone from the Resistance," protested Jan's mother.

"My orders are to search every house in the town. Even stupid orders have to be obeyed."

"We've nothing to hide," she replied. "Go ahead, waste your time."

While the two soldiers were searching, Jan raced over to Elli's house.

"Elli, the Germans are searching every house in the town looking for Resistance fighters and boys avoiding going to the work camps in Germany."

"We must write notes. We know who's working against the Germans," cried Elli. "We'll push the notes under their doors and then ring the bell and run. That way, we'll know they get the notes quickly."

"And no-one will suspect it was us," said Jan.

As fast as they could, the two of them wrote the warnings and then ran through the town, posting the notes, ringing the doorbells and then running as they had planned.

Chapter 9
Suspicion

Spring came and it got warmer and there were blue skies again. But still there was very little food and everyone looked thin and ill.

Sometimes the Germans gave Jan's father a bit of meat. It was cooked in a soup with potatoes and carrots and had to last for days.

Major Konrad came to eat with them one evening, bringing with him some oranges.

Jan's mouth watered. "I haven't had oranges since before the war," he said.

"Ah, well, you Dutch are so stupid. You are happy that railwaymen go on strike. And now you complain that you're starving. It's all your own fault," replied the Major grimly.

Jan decided he hated Major Konrad so much he wouldn't eat an orange.

"Yes, you Dutch have proved very stubborn and difficult," Major Konrad went on, "and there is a traitor somewhere among you. We must find him and punish him."

"What do you mean?" said Jan's father in surprise.

"You know how it's been, Bakker. Every time we go after the Resistance fighters and the Jews, they vanish. It's not chance.

56

Someone is warning them in advance when a search is planned."

Jan's guts turned to jelly. "Do you have any idea who it is?" he asked.

"I've a pretty good idea," replied the Major grimly. "Have an orange, Jan, they're good."

Shaking, Jan took the orange. If the Major suspected him, it was not a good idea to refuse his gift.

As soon as he could, Jan rushed over to Elli's house. "Major Konrad knows that people are being warned when a search is coming," he told her. "He says he has an idea of who it is and he gave me a nasty look."

"Does he think it's *you*?" breathed Elli.

"I think so," nodded Jan.

"You'll have to be careful. I'd better deliver the warnings alone from now on."

"They may suspect you too," Jan pointed out, "the risk is the same for both of us."

"No, they won't," argued Elli. "The Nazis don't think girls do such things and everyone in this town thinks I'm a wimp. I'm the perfect person for the job. And listen. I overheard my father talking on the phone today and there is something we have to do at once."

"What?" demanded Jan.

"We have to go and warn Pieter that the Police are coming to arrest him. They know he's involved in the Resistance."

"Good," said Jan, "serve him right. I hate Pieter. He's made my life miserable for years. Let them arrest him. I'm not going to risk my life for him." And he put on his coat and made for the door.

Elli stood between Jan and the door and shouted at him. "Jan, stop it. You sound like a Nazi. Just remember we're on the side of the Resistance."

"But Elli, Pieter has bullied you too. How can you care what happens to him?"

"Because he's a human being. Of course he's angry with the Germans and anyone who has anything to do with them. His father was shot and is in a labour camp, remember? This war has done terrible things to all of us. Of course he hates us. He thinks we're on the same side as his father's killers. In his shoes, you'd feel just the same."

Jan blushed. "I hadn't thought of that, Elli, you're right. But it's very hard to care about people who hate you."

"I know," agreed Elli. "Now you write the note and I'll get ready to go out and chuck it through Pieter's window."

Jan wrote in capital letters:

GET OUT! THE POLICE ARE COMING FOR YOU TONIGHT!

"Good," said Elli, "now give it to me and go home." Elli ran down the street with the note in her pocket.

Jan set out for home and then thought to himself, *I must make sure she's all right. I'll follow her.*

Jan followed Elli through the deserted streets until they came to Pieter's house. Jan could see Pieter's mother through the window.

Elli picked up a stone, wrapped the note round it and threw it at the window, which broke.

But to his horror, Jan saw that the note had fallen off and blown across the street. Jan raced to fetch it. He tore it into tiny bits and let the wind scatter them before anyone could read it.

Just then the door of the house flew open and Pieter's mother rushed out. Elli ran but the woman was too fast for her and grabbed her.

"You little Nazi lover," she shouted, twisting Elli's arm. "Breaking decent people's windows!"

Jan ran up, "It's all my fault," he told the angry woman. "I dared her to do it. Your Pieter has made us both miserable for long enough. I'm glad the Germans are coming for him today. He deserves everything he gets."

Pieter's mother turned white when Jan said that. She raced back into the house. "Well, we gave her the message," said Elli smiling.

"But we're in trouble now," nodded Jan.

Chapter 10
Arrested

Elli and Jan walked back to Jan's place. Jan's mother was at the door, waiting for them in tears.

"How could you two do that?" she shouted. "As if we aren't in enough trouble. This war will be over any day now and we've been on the wrong side."

Jan caught Elli's eye and thought, *we haven't been on the wrong side*.

"How could you go breaking windows?" Jan's mother continued.

"It wasn't Jan, it was me," Elli told her.

"But I dared her," added Jan.

Just then they heard a knock at the door and there stood Private Stern.

"Sorry, Mrs Bakker, but I've been told I've got to bring these two children into Headquarters. There are a few questions we need to ask them. In fact, they're in trouble."

"What – for breaking windows?"

"We have to keep up law and order, or so my betters tell me. Come on, Elli and Jan, this won't take long."

As the three of them walked to the Police Headquarters, Jan asked, "What's going to happen to us?"

"You'll have to wait and see," he replied in a quiet voice. "Now listen, you two. I know what you've been up to and I don't blame you. I'd have done the same myself. This vile war is almost over, only days to go, I'd say. There's no point in more killing. So just say you're sorry. Tell them you didn't mean trouble. Then go home and stay there till it's all over. Don't try to be heroes, OK?"

"Why are you protecting us?" demanded Elli. "We're not on the same side."

"Oh yes, we are," said Private Stern, "we're longing for this hell to be over. I've fought in two wars now and all they bring is death and destruction and misery. My sons both died in Russia. My wife is homeless in Germany with our daughter and her children.

What's the good in that? So keep your mouths shut and I won't betray you. Let's all pray to God that it's over soon."

Elli and Jan stared at Private Stern.

"So you're surprised? Don't be. Germans are not all monsters. I never agreed with Hitler, I never joined the Nazi Party and there are many like me – ordinary men and women who just want to get on with their lives. But Major Konrad's a real Nazi, just be very polite, tell him how sorry and ashamed you are and pretend to be scared."

"I *am* scared," Jan told him.

"So much the better," nodded Private Stern, as they arrived at the Police Headquarters. "Now remember, don't try to be heroes."

Chapter 11
Hitler's Dead

Jan and Elli were left sitting outside Major Konrad's room for ages.

"He always does this," Jan whispered to Elli. "Dad told me he does it just to make people even more scared."

"Well, it works, doesn't it?" Elli whispered back. "I'm shaking all over."

Suddenly the door burst open and there stood Major Konrad with a black look on his face. "All right, you two, come in. No, I've changed my mind. Maybe I'll take you in one at a time. Miss Elli first."

"Thank you, Major Konrad," said Elli meekly, as she walked into the room. The door slammed behind her.

Jan felt sick as he waited, he could hear Major Konrad shouting. *Was this just about a broken window*, thought Jan, *or did Major Konrad really know something*?

Finally, Elli was pushed out of the room. Jan could see she had been crying. Briefly, Jan caught her eye and saw her shake her head. Then Major Konrad yelled, "All right, Young Bakker, your turn now."

Remembering what Private Stern had said, Jan stood with his head down, trying to look ashamed of himself.

"Right," snarled Major Konrad. "I know it all. You and your girlfriend have been warning Jews and Resistance fighters, telling them when we are going to conduct a search. That's how they escape us. That's how they get away."

Jan thought, *Major Konrad is just saying this to make me give our secret away. He knows nothing, for sure. Elli hasn't told him.*

"Oh, no," cried Jan. "Why would Elli and I do that? After all, our families are on *your* side."

"Well, the war won't last forever. Maybe you're afraid you backed the wrong side? Maybe you want to make sure you won't be in trouble if us Nazis return to Germany and leave you to face the Resistance?"

Jan's heart leapt. All these questions. So Major Konrad didn't know the truth. It was all bluff.

"Oh, no, Major, I don't feel like that at all. I mean, my father has been working for you all through the war. No-one in the Resistance would believe a word we said."

"That makes sense," growled the Major. "But someone tipped off the Jews hiding in the hut. And someone told everyone that we were coming to search people's houses. If it's not you and your girlfriend, Elli, who is it?"

A cloud of relief swept across Jan, the Major had definitely been bluffing. He had been trying to catch them out.

"I don't know, Major," said Jan humbly, "but whoever it is, I do hope you find them soon."

"I will, don't you worry, I will. Now off you go and don't break any more windows. I don't need Pieter's mother in here again. That woman yelled at me for an hour complaining about you. She's no friend of yours, I can tell you."

"No, Sir. Well, I hate Pieter. He picks on Elli and me all the time. We wish you'd put him in prison, Sir, we really do."

"Good. Well, off you go now and no more stone throwing."

Shaking all over, Jan walked through the German Headquarters. He passed a room where a group of soldiers were hunched over a radio. Jan stopped for a moment and heard a voice saying, "Our great and glorious leader Adolf Hitler is dead. He died in the course of his duty. Long live Germany ..." then they played the German national anthem. Jan noticed that many of the soldiers had tears running down their face.

The war is almost over, thought Jan as he raced out into the street to find Elli and tell her the wonderful news.

Chapter 12
The Truth is Told

Jan and Elli decided to follow Private Stern's advice and to stay at home for a few days. One moment the town was silent and then, a second later, everyone seemed to spill out onto the street.

"The Germans have surrendered!" they were shouting.

"The war is over!"

"The British are almost here ..."

"Peace at last!"

That night, a huge bonfire was lit in the centre of the town. The town band came out and played, while people danced and sang.

In Jan's small room, Jan and Elli listened to the music and smelled the sweet scent of the burning wood.

"Come on, Jan," cried Elli. "We can celebrate too. Come on, let's dance, just the two of us." And they danced round and round laughing with relief and pleasure.

Then, as suddenly as it had begun, the music stopped.

"What's happening?" asked Elli, as they leaned out of the window as far as they could.

"Listen, it's tanks," cried Jan, "I can hear them."

"Are the Germans coming back?" asked Elli anxiously.

"No, it's the British. Everyone's cheering. Look – there's Pieter. He's sitting up on one of the tanks. They're British tanks – the British are here to set us free."

A huge cheer went up. Women grabbed flowers from the window boxes and threw them up at the men on the tanks, who threw cigarettes back. Elli and Jan cheered too. Tears of joy were running down their faces.

"Oh, Jan," said Elli, "this is the happiest moment of my life."

"Mine too," agreed Jan. "But remember, to everyone else, we're still the children of Nazi lovers. We still won't be accepted."

"I don't care," said Elli, "I know, and you know, that we did our bit to help the Resistance."

Then there was a loud knock at the door. Jan leaned out. "It's the Dutch police," he told Elli.

"They must have come for your father," she replied.

"Jan," came his mother's voice, "come down at once."

Jan ran downstairs. His mother's face was pale and she was crying. "They've come to take your father away. Say goodbye to him."

Jan looked at his father, standing there in handcuffs, looking small and scared. "Goodbye, Dad. Come back soon," he said and tried hard to smile.

"Bye, son, take care of your mother. Do your best. I'll be thinking of you."

"Enough of that, Bakker. Think about all the men you handed over to the Germans. What happened to their wives and children? Now, move on, you creep. Prison's too good for you," said a police officer.

****

Life went on much the same for Jan and Elli. No-one would speak to them. No-one wanted to know them. Only Ruth, the daughter of the Jewish dentist was kind. She was back in their class.

"It's not Elli's and Jan's fault that their fathers were traitors," she told the others, "Just as it wasn't my fault that my father was a Jew."

Elli and Jan smiled gratefully, but her words made no difference.

Then the word went around that Ruth and her family were going to leave and start a new life in America.

"Let's send her a good luck card," suggested Jan. "She's been so nice to us."

"Great idea," agreed Elli, "I'll make one and we can both sign it."

So Elli made a card and she and Jan wrote:

To our friend Ruth, the only one who tried to understand. Good luck and much happiness

They both signed it and then went down to the train station to give it to her.

The whole town was there on the platform to say goodbye to the Steins. Jan and Elli had to push their way through the crowd to reach Ruth. Jan handed her the card. She opened it and a look of surprise came over her face.

"Jan," she called. "Jan Bakker, I recognise your writing. So it was you who warned us that the Germans were going to search the wood. It was *you*. It was, wasn't it?"

Jan blushed.

"Was it, was it?" demanded Ruth and Dr Stein.

"Yes, it was," shouted Elli. "You and lots of others. Jan risked his life for you."

"Not just me," said Jan, "Elli too. It was Elli who threw the stone through your window, Pieter."

"You were trying to warn us," gasped Pieter amazed.

"We DID warn you," said Elli.

"Let's get this right. Are you saying that you used the information from your fathers to warn us?" asked Pieter.

Jan and Elli nodded.

The train began to move.

"Jan and Elli, thank you, and God bless you," shouted Ruth as the train pulled out. "And I hope everyone will understand what you did. You were heroes. You saved our lives."

There was a silence in the crowd as the train vanished into the distance.

Barrington Stoke was a famous and much-loved story-teller. He travelled from village to village carrying a lantern to light his way. He arrived as it grew dark and when the young boys and girls of the village saw the glow of his lantern, they hurried to the central meeting place. They were full of excitement and expectation, for his stories were always wonderful.

Then Barrington Stoke set down his lantern. In the flickering light the listeners were enthralled by his tales of adventure, horror and mystery. He knew exactly what they liked best and he loved telling a good story. And another. And then another. When the lantern burned low and dawn was nearly breaking, he slipped away. He was gone by morning, only to appear the next day in some other village to tell the next story.

Barrington Stoke would like to thank all its readers for commenting on the manuscript before publication and in particular:

Lauren Blane
Christopher Bond
Rebecca Cleary
Hannah Cronshaw
Ben Cronshaw
Jimmi Davson
Jenny Gooch
K. Hewitt
Rory Hollands
Imran Khan
D. Leddy
Fay Marsden
Louise Marshall
Jena Mathews

Liam McMain
Dean Methven
Rachel Moody
Daniel Reid
Anne Robins
Philip Roe
Brenda Scales
Oliver Spearpoint
Daniel Spencer
Jason Springall
Tom Swatridge
Robbie Throup
Faye Troy

Barrington Stoke Club

Would you like to become a member of our club? Children who write to us with their views become members of our club and special advisors to the company. They also have the chance to act as editors on future manuscripts. Contact us at the address or website below – we'd love to hear from you!

Barrington Stoke, 10 Belford Terrace, Edinburgh EH4 3DQ
Tel: 0131 315 4933 Fax: 0131 315 4934
E-mail: info@barringtonstoke.co.uk
Website: www.barringtonstoke.co.uk

If you loved this story, why don't you read . . .

Bungee Hero

by Julie Bertagna

Are you afraid of heights? Adam is terrified of them. So why then would he do a bungee jump to earn money for charity? It is only after Mr Haddock tells him his sad story that Adam decides to take the plunge. But will he just be too scared to do it?

You can order this book directly from:
Macmillan Distribution Ltd, Brunel Road, Houndmills,
Basingstoke, Hampshire RG21 6XS
Tel: 01256 302699

If you loved this story, why don't you read . . .

Second Chance

by Alison Prince

Have you ever wondered who lived in your house before you? When Ross and his family have to leave their house, their new home is an old café by the sea. But who is the boy watching Ross? Watching, and waiting?

You can order this book directly from:
Macmillan Distribution Ltd, Brunel Road, Houndmills,
Basingstoke, Hampshire RG21 6XS
Tel: 01256 302699